TALES FROM SCHROON LAKE

A Visit from Rudy Beaver

WRITTEN BY

Barbara Davoll

Pictures by Dennis Hockerman

MOODY

To Jack Wyrtzen, encourager and fellow-laborer in the gospel, whose consistent, godly life and ministry at Word of Life International has written the real *"Tales from Schroon Lake"* and has brought our little dot on the map to the attention of the world.

"This book of the law shall not depart out of thy mouth, but thou shalt meditate therein day and night, that thou mayest observe to do according to all that is written therein; for then thou shalt make thy way prosperous, and then thou shalt have good success."
Joshua 1:8

Moody Press, a ministry of the Moody Bible Institute, is designed for education, evangelization, and edification. If we may assist you in knowing more about Christ and the Christian life, please write us without obligation: Moody Press, c/o MLM, Chicago, IL 60610.

ISBN: 0-8024-1034-0
13579108642
Printed in the United States of America

"Tales From Schroon Lake," is the newest animal adventure series for children written by Barbara Davoll. It takes its setting from the tiny town of Schroon Lake, high in the Adirondack Mountains of upstate New York, where Barbara and her husband, Roy, make their home and serve the Lord with Word of Life International as Children's Representatives. The Davolls are lovingly known around the world as "Uncle Roy and Aunt Barb" as they minister in children's crusades at home and abroad.

Barbara is well known for her award-winning, best-selling Christopher Churchmouse Classics and the Molehole Mystery series. She has allowed her many talents and abilities to be used for the Lord in the areas of writing, composing, teaching, and music, but she loves being a wife, mother, and grandmother and still enjoys being a homemaker for Roy and their schnauzer, Josh.

Illustrator Dennis Hockerman collaborated with friend Barbara Davoll to bring to life a family of lovable churchmice, a captivating underground village of moles, and now a charming band of beavers. Balancing fun-filled imagery with the natural realism of life in a beaver lodge proved to be a real challenge in creating the "Tales From Schroon Lake" series. The artist enjoys viewing the world through a child's eyes and works almost exclusively in the children's market. He lives with his wife, three children, and two Yorkshire terriers in Mequon, Wisconsin, a Milwaukee suburb.

Bucky Beaver and his little cousin,
Rudy, swam slowly up Schroon Lake to the
area known as Beaver Falls. They looked like two
logs as they swam side by side. Only their noses were
above the water. Suddenly, Bucky made a nosedive. Rudy
followed and was quick enough to see his older cousin enter
the beaver lodge.

Inside, Bucky sat back on his haunches and started to comb his fur with his long nails. "You'd better comb your fur, Rudy," he advised. "It won't be waterproofed if you don't."

"Naw, not me," the lazy beaver yawned. "I'm going to take a nice little snappy nappy. This has been a big day." And with that he sprawled out on his bunk and fell asleep. He began to snore quietly.

Bucky stared at his sleeping cousin. *He's really something else,* thought Bucky with disgust. Bucky didn't like to comb himself each day either, but he knew it was necessary. *Sometimes you have to do stuff just because it's right,* he thought.

He was learning a lot about Rudy since he'd come to stay with Bucky's family. *I can see why they named him "Rudy,"* he thought as he raked his shining fur with his big nails. *He's rude and lazy, and we're stuck with him for two weeks.* Bucky sighed gloomily and continued his combing.

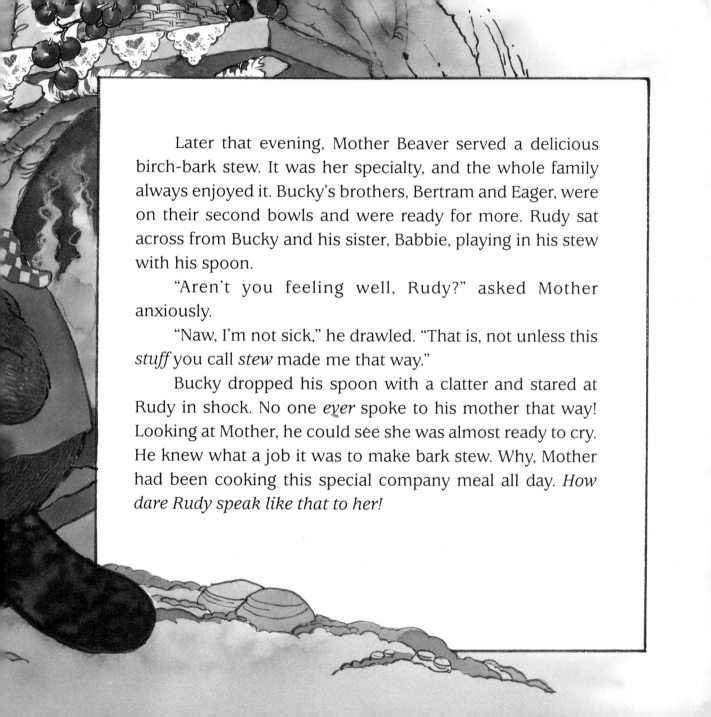

Later that evening, Mother Beaver served a delicious birch-bark stew. It was her specialty, and the whole family always enjoyed it. Bucky's brothers, Bertram and Eager, were on their second bowls and were ready for more. Rudy sat across from Bucky and his sister, Babbie, playing in his stew with his spoon.

"Aren't you feeling well, Rudy?" asked Mother anxiously.

"Naw, I'm not sick," he drawled. "That is, not unless this *stuff* you call *stew* made me that way."

Bucky dropped his spoon with a clatter and stared at Rudy in shock. No one *ever* spoke to his mother that way! Looking at Mother, he could see she was almost ready to cry. He knew what a job it was to make bark stew. Why, Mother had been cooking this special company meal all day. *How dare Rudy speak like that to her!*

Father cleared his throat. "We don't speak that way to Mother, Rudy," he rebuked gently. "She has worked hard making this good meal, and we are thankful, aren't we, children?

"It's great!" said Bertram.

"Super," said Eager. "It's my favorite meal. Mom can really cook!"

Babbie, whose mouth was full, nodded her head in agreement.

"Perhaps Rudy isn't used to eating bark stew," soothed Mother, trying to smile. "What do you usually eat at home, dear?"

"Nothing but *aspen* leaves and bark," said the snooty beaver with his nose in the air. "We *never* eat birch if we can help it."

"I'm afraid we'd be hungry here in the mountains if we only ate aspen." Father laughed. "Aspen trees are few and far between. You'll have to get used to birch, I guess."

"I *suppose* I can eat it if I have to," grumped Rudy, shoving a spoonful into his mouth. He noisily began slurping the stew as the entire family watched with disgust.

"You're rude!" snapped Babbie, glaring at him.

"That's my name–*Rudy* Beaver," replied the impossible cousin with pride.

Mother Beaver gave a warning glance at her daughter to be quiet. What Babbie had said was true, but Mother didn't want a quarrel to develop. Babbie was known for being very outspoken.

"Use your napkin," whispered Bucky.

"What for?" The rude beaver snorted. "Will that make it taste better?"

Mother drew in her breath sharply and looked away from him.

"Will you excuse us, Rudy?" said Father, getting up from his place with dignity.

"I'm sure you can finish without us." And with that, the entire family left the visiting beaver sitting at the table alone.

"Well, of all the nerve!" Rudy snapped angrily. "Some way to treat your company his *first night* here!"

"What a pain he is," whispered Bertram to Eager and Bucky as they went into the living room.

Babbie had her paw around Mother Beaver's arm. She loved her mother and didn't like to see her upset.

"He'd better lay off talking like that to my mother," stormed Bucky. "Or he won't have any front teeth to chew his aspen!"

"Children," responded Father sharply. "We'll not have any of that talk. Rudy is our guest, and we *will not* lower ourselves by speaking in nasty ways about him. He obviously needs some help. Perhaps we can teach him some manners."

Bucky rolled his eyes and said no more. When Father spoke like that, he meant business. But his cousin was a terrible beaver and would have to share his room. Somehow Bucky knew that would not be easy.

After supper Bucky, his brothers, and Rudy swam ashore and went to the Beaver Falls sandlot to play ball. Razzy Raccoon, Sniffer Skunk, and other beaver boys were there to play. Several times Rudy nearly got into a fight when Peter Packrat, the umpire, made a close call. Bucky was glad when the game was over and they could go home. It was no fun playing ball with his visiting cousin.

The boys were getting ready for bed when Bucky remembered he had loaned Rudy his baseball glove.

"Where's my glove?"

"I thought *you* had it," said Rudy lazily.

"No way," Bucky responded. "I let you use it."

"Yeah," his cousin drawled. "But I thought you'd bring it home. It's *your* glove."

"Rudy! I had my *other* glove. When you borrow something, you usually bring it back."

"Not me," snapped Rudy. "I don't carry anything that's not mine."

"Oh, for crying out loud! That was my best glove. I *knew* I shouldn't let you play with it. Where did you leave it?"

"Out under the trees by third base," said Rudy with little interest. "We can get it in the morning," he yawned.

"Not on your life! We'll go now!" said the determined Bucky.

"All that way? Are you crazy?"

"No! Just mad!" he whispered, remembering his family was already in bed.

Ten minutes later the beavers pulled themselves up out of the water onto the Beaver Falls wharf. "Let's go!" said Bucky urgently. "Mom won't like us out here this time of night."

"Aw, don't be such a sissy," responded his cousin.

After a bit of searching, they found the glove, and started toward home. As they were scampering over the wharf, Rudy let out a low whistle. "Hey, Buck! Look over here. What's in these cans?"

Bucky turned to see his cousin perched on top of a wharf garbage can. Two other gleaming cans stood nearby. Bucky knew they had just been purchased by the town leaders. He also knew that the animals had been given strict rules by Peter Packrat, their sheriff.

Peter was a good sport, but he had been very stern when he had talked to them about the new garbage cans. "Now, I know you guys, especially the raccoons, love to get into garbage. But we're going to ask you not to do that anymore. It isn't healthy, and it makes a real mess. These cans are off limits for the Beaver Falls baseball team."

Bucky remembered all this now. But by the time he got to Rudy, his wild cousin had the lid off one can and was throwing garbage out on the wharf.

"Whee! Look at this!" he yelled. "Humans throw away such good stuff. Look at these steak bones. There's a full beaver meal in here!" Rudy climbed into the can and began gnawing hungrily on a bone.

In spite of himself, Bucky could see that Rudy had a real find. Bucky looked both ways. There were no lights anywhere in town. Even Peter Packrat was asleep. Surely it would be all right just this once. Bucky jumped up on the can and grabbed a bone himself. This was so easy and so good.

The next afternoon Rudy called Bucky aside. "Hey, Buck! Wasn't that great last night? Why don't we take a little swim tonight—you know—just to cool off. And then we might get ourselves a little snack on the wharf again before turning in. What do you say?"

Bucky grinned at his cousin. Today had been a better day than yesterday. Rudy had almost seemed nice. *Maybe if I do this we'll get along better,* Bucky reasoned. *Mom and Dad will never have to know.*

And so began a pattern for the two weeks Rudy stayed with Bucky. Each night they waited until all were asleep and then made the trip to the Beaver Falls wharf. Bucky often felt guilty when he saw Peter or the town leaders. But he told himself that they really weren't doing anything wrong. The garbage was stuff the humans didn't want. And it was just for two weeks anyway.

The last night as they hopped up on the wharf, Rudy was unusually frisky. "Come on, Buck! Don't be such a slow-mo. Let's get to it! " He jumped up on the cans and began throwing off the lids, making more noise than usual.

"Shhh!" warned Bucky.

"Don't shhh me," Rudy chuckled. "Wait till you see what I've got planned for tonight!"

Bucky watched with fear growing in his heart. Rudy was throwing garbage all over the wharf. He'd never been this reckless before. What if some of the townspeople woke up and came to investigate?

"Rudy! Stop!" screamed Bucky. "We can never clean this up! What are you doing?"

"Come on, cuz! Get with the action. This is fun. These old long-beards won't know what hit their town!" And with that, Rudy jumped off the can and started rolling it down the wharf toward Peter Packrat's house. Garbage was flying everywhere.

"Rudy! Are you crazy? That's Peter Packrat's house!"

"You think I don't know?" yelled the out-of-control beaver wildly. "That old rat put me out in too many games.

We'll see how he likes chicken bones and pig feed all over his porch." Rudy dumped one can and started back for another. "This old guy is a packrat. Let's see if he'll pack up this stuff. It's fit for a rat!"

Just then the light flew on in Peter's house, and the old rat stepped out the door. He was comical to see wearing his three night hats and two ties. He was a packrat all right. But when Bucky saw him, he felt sick. Peter had been so kind to the animal boys.

Bucky took a flying leap off the dock and dove to the bottom of the lake. He didn't want to be caught doing those awful things to Peter. Then he saw a form racing toward him underwater. Rudy was making his getaway too. The beavers swam furiously to Bucky's lodge.

"I'm *glad* you're going home tomorrow," whispered Bucky angrily as he got into bed. "You've made our name like mud in town."

"Aw, relax, cuz! You just get too upset over everything," Rudy said. "They won't find out." And he was right. They didn't. At least not then.

One day, several weeks after his cousin left, Bucky's family received a letter from Rudy's father. It said that ever since Rudy's visit, he had been sneaking out at night. One night he had been caught stealing things. His parents knew he wasn't always good, but he had never stolen before. Rudy's father said he hoped he had been a good beaver while he was visiting them.

"Oh, I'm so glad he didn't get into trouble while he was here," said Mother Beaver.

"Well, he *was* a problem but at least..." Father was interrupted by a sound from Bucky.

The little beaver had his head down and was crying.

"Why, Bucky, I'm sure we all feel terrible about Rudy, but we really can't help it that he got into trouble," Father said kindly. Bucky tearfully moved closer to his father.

"Oh, but Father, it's all my fault!"

"Why, how so?" asked Father, puzzled.

Bucky gulped and tried to talk through his tears. "From the first night he was here he–he and I went out at night and got into the garbage cans on the wharf. I thought it was all right because it was stuff thrown away. But the last night..." Bucky's voice broke, and he could hardly tell the story.

Bucky's family looked shocked. It was hard to believe that Bucky, who had always been such a good beaver, was responsible for the awful mess in town. It was a very long night for Bucky as he tried to explain all that had happened during Rudy's visit.

"And so I *am* to blame, aren't I?" finished Bucky.

Father's usually kind face was very stern. "I'm afraid you are, Bucky. Although you didn't dump any trash on Peter's house, you were there. That makes you a part of it. You set the wrong example for Rudy by going with him. If you couldn't stop him, you should have come and told me," said Father sadly.

"What can I do, Father?" cried Bucky. He had never felt so bad in his entire life.

"Well, the first thing you must do is go to Peter Packrat and the town leaders and explain to them what happened. Then you will have to go to work and pay for the damages to Peter's house. You must also write to Rudy and apologize for the poor example you set by letting him think it was all right to go out at night and make trouble."

Bucky looked at his parents, brothers, and Babbie. He knew he had disappointed them greatly. But he was ready and anxious to make things right. He had learned some valuable lessons. Most important, he had learned how not to be a rude beaver.

BUCKY'S

BELIEVE IT OR NOT

Beavers walk on their hind legs and use their paws like hands. They seem very humanlike in their actions.

Beavers construct their dams, sometimes in just one night, making small streams into ponds and lakes.

When there is danger nearby, beavers slap the water with their wide, flat tails. This sound can be heard even under the water.

A beaver lodge, usually built in the middle of a pond, has a front door and a back door. The doors are underwater, but you can see the top of the lodge in the middle of the pond.
Beavers work mostly at night. They are afraid of people. They can overcome this fear, but it takes a long time.

BEAVER TAILS

Rudy Beaver visited Bucky for two weeks. At that time Bucky learned some valuable lessons. Bucky knew that Rudy was not a well-behaved beaver. He should not have listened to his cousin when Rudy wanted to sneak out at night.

Instead of being a good example to Rudy, Bucky followed him. This led Rudy to do even worse things at home.

Sometimes children are just like Bucky. They *know* to do right, but instead they follow their friends and get into trouble. There is a verse in God's Word that is good for us to remember. It says:

Don't let anyone think little of you because you are young. Be their ideal [or example]; let them follow the way you teach and live; be a pattern for them in your love, your faith and your clean thoughts" / 1 Timothy 4:12, *The Living Bible*.

We should always try to be a good example for our friends. In that way we will be teaching what is right by the way we live. What kind of pattern are you?